Dear Parents:

T5-CVF-038

Congratulations! Your child is taking the first steps on an exciting journey. The destination? Independent reading!

STEP INTO READING® will help your child get there. The program offers five steps to reading success. Each step includes fun stories and colorful art or photographs. In addition to original fiction and books with favorite characters, there are Step into Reading Non-Fiction Readers, Phonics Readers and Boxed Sets, Sticker Readers, and Comic Readers—a complete literacy program with something to interest every child.

Learning to Read, Step by Step!

Ready to Read   Preschool–Kindergarten
• big type and easy words • rhyme and rhythm • picture clues
For children who know the alphabet and are eager to begin reading.

Reading with Help   Preschool–Grade 1
• basic vocabulary • short sentences • simple stories
For children who recognize familiar words and sound out new words with help.

Reading on Your Own   Grades 1–3
• engaging characters • easy-to-follow plots • popular topics
For children who are ready to read on their own.

Reading Paragraphs   Grades 2–3
• challenging vocabulary • short paragraphs • exciting stories
For newly independent readers who read simple sentences with confidence.

Ready for Chapters   Grades 2–4
• chapters • longer paragraphs • full-color art
For children who want to take the plunge into chapter books but still like colorful pictures.

STEP INTO READING® is designed to give every child a successful reading experience. The grade levels are only guides; children will progress through the steps at their own speed, developing confidence in their reading.

Remember, a lifetime love of reading starts with a single step!

Copyright © 2024 Disney Enterprises, Inc. All rights reserved. Published in the United States by Random House Children's Books, a division of Penguin Random House LLC, 1745 Broadway, New York, NY 10019, and in Canada by Penguin Random House Canada Limited, Toronto, in conjunction with Disney Enterprises, Inc.

Step into Reading, Random House, and the Random House colophon are registered trademarks of Penguin Random House LLC.

Visit us on the Web!
rhcbooks.com

Educators and librarians, for a variety of teaching tools, visit us at RHTeachersLibrarians.com

ISBN 978-0-7364-4456-9 (trade) — ISBN 978-0-7364-9048-1 (lib. bdg.)
ISBN 978-0-7364-4457-6 (ebook)

Printed in the United States of America

10 9 8 7 6 5 4 3 2 1

Random House Children's Books supports the First Amendment and celebrates the right to read.

DISNEY
ENCANTO

The Missing Sound

by Susana Illera Martínez

adapted by Nicole Johnson

illustrated by the

Disney Storybook Art Team

Random House 🏠 New York

Dolores Madrigal has
a special gift.
She can hear everything!
She loves listening to
the sounds of
the Encanto.

Dolores wakes up
one morning.
She can hear the coffee
brewing in the kitchen.

She can hear
her brother Camilo
and her cousin Luisa.
They race down the stairs.

Dolores goes into
the hallway.
She hears her cousin
Isabela dropping
flower petals.

She hears her cousin
Mirabel sewing in
her room.

Dolores eats breakfast.
She hears the birds
flying in the sky.

She hears Don Osvaldo
feeding his chickens.

She hears the kids
playing in the street.
But a sound is missing.

Dolores talks to her mom,
Pepa, and Abuela.
She tells them about
the missing sound.

Something is wrong
in the Encanto!
They know she can fix
the problem.

Dolores asks her brother
and cousins for help.
She leans out
the window.

She listens to
the sounds of
the Encanto.

Dolores leads
her family outside.
They walk through
the town.

They greet Don Osvaldo
and his donkey.
Dolores thinks the
missing sound is nearby.

Dolores walks toward
the chicken coop.
She listens closely.

"It's here!" she shouts.
The chicken coop is
missing a sound.

Dolores and Mirabel
look at the chickens.
Most of them laid
eggs this morning.
But one chicken looks
a little sick.
She did not lay an
egg like the other
chickens did.

Dolores and Don Osvaldo make a medicine for the sick chicken.

They give the chicken
the medicine.
Soon, she lays an egg!

The chicken is better.
Hooray for Dolores
and her special gift!